STECK-VAUGHN

PAIR-IT BOOKS™

A New Nest

Written by Stephanie Handwerker
Illustrated by Toby Williams

STECK-VAUGHN
C O M P A N Y
ELEMENTARY • SECONDARY • ADULT • LIBRARY

Red robin

2

Tan twigs

3

Yellow yarn

Green grass

Blue beads

6

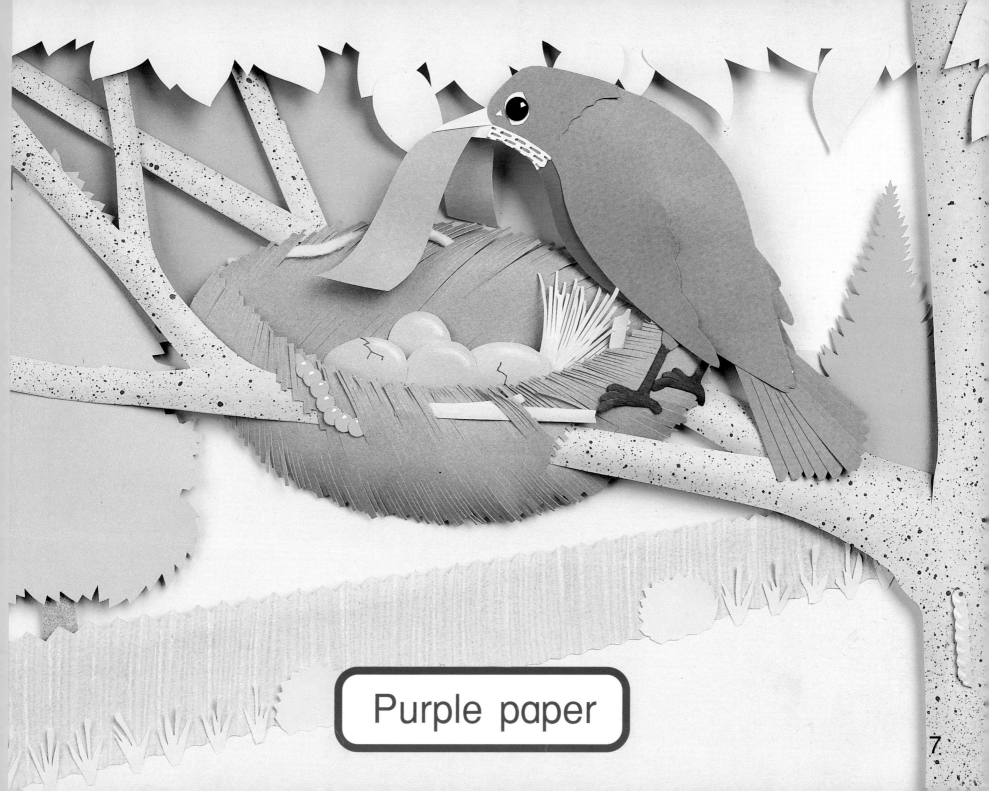

Purple paper

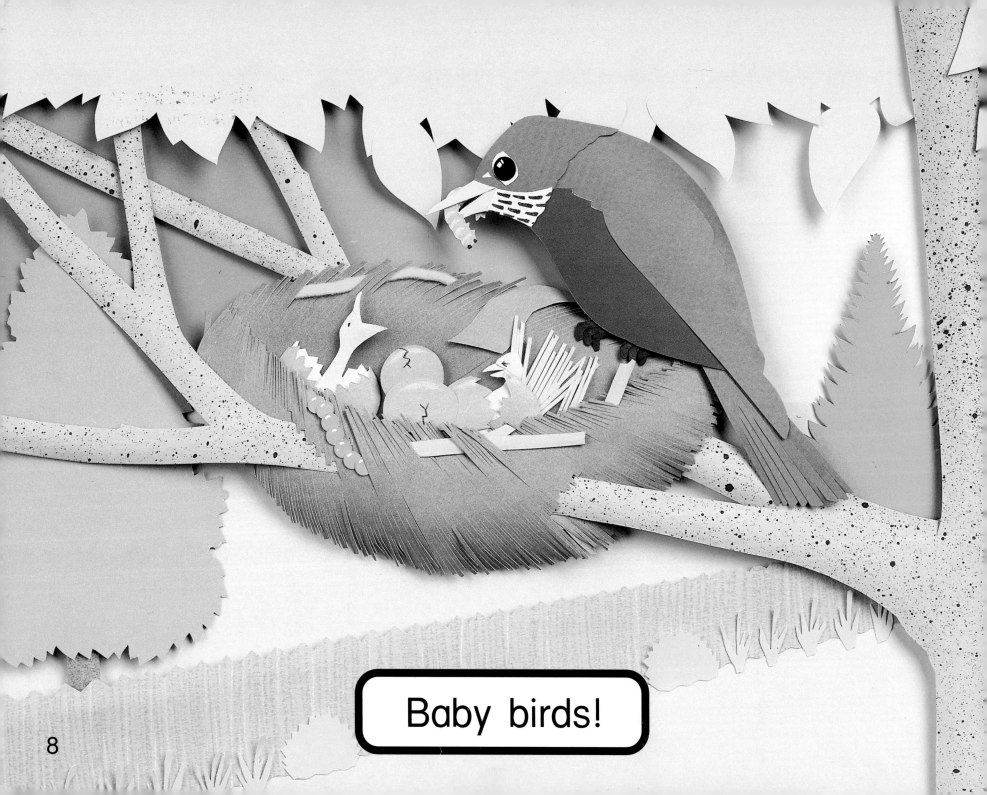

Baby birds!